The SPRING RABBIT

Joyce Dunbar   Susan Varley

Andersen Press

All the little rabbits that lived in the wood
had brothers and sisters. All except Smudge.
"Why haven't I got a sister or a brother?" he
asked his mother.
"Wait until the spring," she answered.

For Jessie Bambridge – J.D
For Michelle and Catherine – S.V

This paperback edition first published in 2014 by Andersen Press Ltd.,
20 Vauxhall Bridge Road, London SW1V 2SA.
Published in Australia by Random House Australia Pty.,
Level 3, 100 Pacific Highway, North Sydney, NSW 2060.
First published in Great Britain in 1994 by Andersen Press.

Colour separated in Switzerland by Photolitho AG, Zürich.
Printed and bound in Singapore by Tien Wah Press.

10   9   8   7   6   5   4   3   2   1

British Library Cataloguing in Publication Data available.
ISBN 978 1 78344 078 8

Spring seemed a long way away.
Smudge watched on a cold autumn morning as the
other rabbits chased falling leaves. Then he had an
idea. He made a leaf rabbit with leafy broken twigs.
"You can be my brother," he said to the leaf rabbit.
"Let's chase each other down the hill."
The leaf rabbit didn't answer.

Then the wind blew all the leaves away
leaving only the bare twigs.
"Wait until the spring," said a mouse.

But spring was a long time coming.
Later, the snow fell. Smudge made a snow rabbit.
"You can be my sister," he said to the snow rabbit.
"Let's have a game of snowball."
But the snow rabbit couldn't play snowball.

Next day, the snow rabbit melted.
"Wait until spring," said a robin.

But spring was a long time coming.
When the snow melted, Smudge made a mud rabbit.
"You can be my brother," he said to the mud rabbit.
"Let's splash about in the puddles."

But the mud rabbit didn't splash about.
The rain came and washed it away.
"Wait until spring," said a frog.

At last came the first signs of spring. All the twigs were sprouting green shoots and the buds were beginning to show.

Smudge went looking for his brother. He looked in the hollows of the trees, but he found no sign of a brother, only a mouse hole, full of baby mice.

"There are no rabbits here," said the mouse.

He looked in the bushes and brambles, but he didn't
find a brother there either, only a bird's nest, with six
speckled eggs.

"There are no rabbits here," said the robin.

He looked in the reeds by the pond, he didn't find
a brother there either only frogspawn full of tiny
tadpoles.
"There are no rabbits here," said the frog.
Smudge felt very sad and lonely. At last he went home.

"I can't find my spring brother anywhere," he said to his mother.

"You were looking in all the wrong places," she said, showing him three tiny bundles. "See what we have here."

Smudge was overjoyed. He had two baby brothers and a sister. As soon as they were hopping about he made them an enormous moss rabbit . . .

. . . and everyone knew that spring had come.

Other books illustrated by Susan Varley:

9781849394093

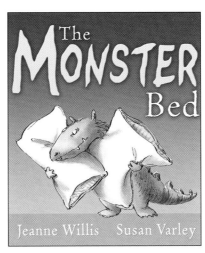

9781842702222

9781849395144

9781842708194

9781842705896